Earthbound Origins

(a side story presents) Project David

Shavor D. Morrison

To my wife & kids!

I love you!

("...and no honey, this is not based on me, I swear!")

2 SAMUEL

CHAPTER 12:7-8

7. —I anointed you as king over Israel, and I spared you from the hand of Saul.

8. I also gave you your master's house, and put your master's wives into your care and under your protection, and I gave you the house (royal dynasty) of Israel and of Judah; and if that had been too little, I would have given you much more!

CHAPTER I

THE NEWCOMER

A Motel 6 lobby window lit up as a vehicle approached, parked, and eventually shut off.

Ironically, the blinds were fully closed while the **OPEN** sign flashed on and off sluggishly, with dull red and blue colors.

There was only one other car in the parking lot beside the newcomers—a beat-up and rusty Honda, which looked incompetent compared to the black, chromed-out Mercedes S.U.V.

The Mercedes was an impressive-looking chariot!

The driver's side door swung open, and a man stepped out dressed as if he had just got off a Harley-Davidson motorcycle and walked into an NWA music video shoot. He wore blue jeans with intentional rips that overlay white sneakers and a white t-shirt covered by a matching blue jacket.
A thick, shiny gold chain dangled from his neck, swinging as he walked.

He approached the lobby door, opening it to reveal a calming and straightforward atmosphere, your typical motel lobby setting. Pictures, plants, the semi-cheap coffee station in the corner, and no customer service presence at the lobby desk.

Only a heavy computer with a screen that flickered and a bell.

Your typical motel lobby setting.

DING!!! DING!!! DING!!!

Immediately, a pimply face youngster emerged from the back in haste, pushing his drooping glasses back upon his face.

He also wore a blue jacket covering his motel uniform.

NEWCOMER
"Hey kid, how have you been?"

KID
"Hi, Mister! I've been good, just you know, working and I'm exercising now! You can't see under this jacket—."

NEWCOMER

"—which is a cool jacket, by the way!"
The youngster's eyes gleamed from the approval
from behind his glasses.

KID

"Really?? I mean (cough, cough) Ya,
this thing, it's alright."

The man smiled.

NEWCOMER

"Josh, right??"

The kid stared with wide eyes, frozen stiff.

NEWCOMER

"Hello? Earth to Josh."

The kid snapped back, shaking his head, and cleared
his throat.

KID

"Ya! You remembered my name. Wow! Yes!
I'm Josh; technically, it's Joshua, but people
call me Josh for short. I don't see the point
of chopping off two letters and calling them
short. I mean, it's *short—er*! But you know?"

Joshua looked over his glasses, raised his brows,
shrugged, and held either end of the break line of his

jacket.

JOSHUA
"Lazy people, am I right?"

NEWCOMER
"Right. I would love to sit here and chat
with you, Joshua, but um—."

JOSHUA
"—oh ya, right! [clears throat] Your wife, she's
already in the room, sir. I need your driver's
license, and you will be ready. Sorry."

The newcomer reached into a pocket inside his
jacket and pulled out his wallet. Then, retrieving
what Joshua asked for, handing over his driver's
license.

JOSHUA
"Thank you! Here you go. Like I said before,
she's already there. Same room as usual.
You and the Mrs. enjoy your evening,
and thank you for using Motel 6!"

He nodded, taking his license back, winking at
Joshua before turning around and walking out.

The newcomer got back into his vehicle, reversed,
then drove off. He went down the motel parking

lot, passing building after building, finding another parking space, and turning off the engine. He pulled down his visor inside the vehicle to look in its mirror. Carefully examining his blemishless ebony skin. His dark brown eyes darted in every direction, looking for out-of-whack details.

But everything was perfect!

Because he was—perfection.

He raised the visor before snatching it back down again. He raised his head and moved his wide nose close to the mirror. No boogers in sight! He slammed the visor closed again and reached over the passenger seat, leaning towards the glove box, opening it, and pulling out some mint spray. He opened his mouth, showing off straight and shiny white teeth, spraying a couple of spritzes.

He got out of the car and went to the motel door.

Motel room #66

He lightly tapped on it with his knuckles, and the door opened slowly.

Standing in the doorway, a stunningly beautiful woman wore a thick robe. Her dark black, wet, and curly hair shined, giving off a fruity smell from her shampoo. She smiled. Her thick lips shimmered from the pink lip gloss, making them look as juicy as her shampoo smelled. Everything about her was ideal, which made her eye-catching. From her tiny button nose the carefully trimmed arched eyebrows above her almond-shaped eyes, high cheekbones, and skin. It was smooth, coconut shell brown, and glowed.

The newcomer and the woman were in a trance, lost in one another's eyes. He leaned in—she did, too. They kissed passionately. She unwrapped her robe, lifting her hands, wrapping them around the back of his head, caressing his black curly hair. The robe hit the carpet as he lifted her off it, carrying her away from the doorway. The spring-hinged door closed quickly in the beginning—then slowly at the end— quietly clicking behind them as they made their way towards the bed.

CHAPTER II
AGENT MAMBA &
AGENT FD LANCE

VOICE OVER EARPIECES

"Okay, you two, our resources told us this *THING* will touchdown in fifteen minutes. So I want us alert and ready when it does! Capturing this thing alive is a top priority. So from here on out, comms quiet except for Agent Mamba and Agent FD Lance and, of course, I."

A black Mercedes four-door sedan with even darker windows was parked in the middle of a dark alleyway. Two people were seated inside, wearing matching black tactical suits, shades, and earpieces. Agent Mamba raised his hand to his earpiece and pressed a button.

AGENT MAMBA

"What are the plans for this *"THING"* once catching it?"

VOICE OVER EARPIECES

"For you two, that is classified. Everyone else cooperating and working on this mission is highly classified. Your job is to apprehend the target." Agent FD Lance leaned back in the driver's seat and rolled her eyes.

AGENT FD LANCE
"Por supuesto que es. "Classified." It always is. Hey guys, go rush into conflict and arrest abnormal beings with strange powers! I need you to bring them in alive even though— THEY'RE TRYING TO KILL YOU! And all she can tell us is, "it's classified." Hmm…"

Agent Mamba in the passenger seat laughed, shaking his head.

AGENT FD LANCE
"What??"

AGENT MAMBA
"You ever notice when you get mad, your accent gets thicker?"

The woman narrowed her eyes and stared at her partner, shaking her head and raising her index finger. Who leaned back with both hands raised innocently, smiling.

AGENT MAMBA
"What?? It's cute and kind of

intimidating—hot mostly.”

AGENT FD LANCE
“Cállate!”

VOICE OVER EARPIECES
“We have less than five minutes. I'm briefly bringing Doctor Tamah in on the comms to review the capturing device and how it works. Doctor Tamah?”

DOCTOR TAMAH
“Um…just speak right into here? Okay, thank you. (Clears throat nervously) Thank you, Director, for this…(clears throat again) opportunity. As you know, I am Dr. Tamah, and as the Director stated, I will be going over the capturing device—and by the way, hi, Agent Mamba! I am such a <u>HUGE</u> fan of your work here at the agency. Oh my God! I mean, the way you put down that ‘Behemoth’ several months ago.”

AGENT MAMBA
“Damn, well, thanks! I assume you are responsible for the gadgets we use on our missions?”

DOCTOR TAMAH
“…y…yes, exactly.”

The Director stood behind Doctor Tamah, staring intensely at the back of her red curly hair.

AGENT MAMBA

"Well, thank you, if it wasn't for your beautiful brain and gorgeous green eyes watching over us...."

DIRECTOR
"What do you not understand about BRIEFLY Doctor Tamah?? We are now 120 seconds away from contact. All the Ph.D.'s in the world but don't understand—."

AGENT FD LANCE
"Don't worry about it, Director; I read the briefing and know how to use the device."

DIRECTOR
"Good. Then Agent FD Lance will take point. Good luck, Agents. May the anointing of the Highest be upon you."

The man in the passenger seat unbuckled his seat belt and opened his door. Before leaving, he looked back to see his partner staring at him angrily and shaking her head. He looked around nervously, then back at her.

AGENT MAMBA
"What??"

AGENT FD LANCE
"Sabes que! Gorgeous green eyes, seriously??"

They exited the car, headed back to the trunk, and popped it open. Inside were various styles of weapons: pistols, SMGs, shotguns, and even a sniper rifle. She bent over, reached deeper inside, grabbed a bag, and pulled it out. She unzipped it, revealing a circular metal device with numerous buttons and a blue binary code engraved around it. In the center was a blue orb with jagged strands of blue and yellow lightning flashing, floating in slow motion, and making a humming noise. Agent FD Lance took the device out of the car with a few weapons.

Agent Mamba grabbed a few guns as well.

Then he began to open his mouth to explain when it started to rain. Shortly after, there was lightning, then thunder.

The agents looked at each other in confusion and silence as Agent FD Lance closed the trunk.

AGENT MAMBA
"Wasn't it just clear skies?? There wasn't
rain in the forecast either!"

His partner shook her head, looking as concerned as he was.

The rain began to come down harsher while the lightning flashed brighter and more frequently, followed by the loudness of thunder.

Whatever this thing was, it was getting closer.

<u>BOOM!</u>

Crackles of lightning struck a nearby dumpster blackening the surface it contacted.

And the ground shook around them.

The two agents drew pistols as lightning struck again a few feet away from their car.

Steam from the rain suddenly became thicker and filled the alleyway. Agent FD Lance holstered her gun and kneeled to zip the duffel bag back up, periodically looking around. Agent Mamba stepped before her as his green laser fanned the thick smoke covering her.

Once she got back up, she tossed the bag over her shoulder, tightening it across her body. She upholstered her gun, and they went deeper into the smoke. Which eventually began to thin out and made the alley somewhat seeable again.

Then they came to a halt, immediately tightening their grip and aiming their guns!

Right in front of them stood an amphibian-like creature with a man-like body covered with navy blue pants that gripped his lower muscular torso and legs. He also wore a matching unbuttoned long, silk-like garment that hung down to his scaly calves. Revealing his broad green chest and bulging abs. He had human-like hands, wearing a gold ring with a substantial encrusted crest on his wedding finger. While his feet were webbed. His face was lizard-like that resembled a Chameleon, with vast and long gills running across either side of his neck.

He stared at the agents as they approached with piercing eyes that moved up and down, side-to-side studying and examining all awhile, scowling.

AGENT MAMBA
"Agent Mamba over to the agency. Do
you see what we're looking at??"

DIRECTOR
"Yes, I see it. What it is, I don't
know. Doctor Tamah??"

DOCTOR TAMAH
"I looked over ancient transcripts and
scrolls and couldn't find anything amongst
any creatures, spirits, or demons."

AGENT FD LANCE
"¡Estupenda! Either way, the mission
is to bring it in, correct??"

AGENT MAMBA
"Hey, umm…lizard man! I don't know why
you're here or what brought you here! But
—we need you to come with us ASAP!"

The lizard man's gills opened, sucking air quickly, then released it slowly, closing them. He glanced over at Agent FD Lance then his eyes widened.

PARTITUS
"My name is Partitus. You will show me <u>AND</u> it, respect as it rolls off your tongue, peasant."

AGENT MAMBA
"Okay, I'm going to shoot him now!"
Agent Mamba's index finger pressed against his gun's trigger, ready to squeeze. Then, without warning, Partitus took a step back, disappearing.

AGENT MAMBA
"Nu-uh! Not today!"

Agent Mamba turned and aimed his gun at some pipes nearby and shot. A massive cloud of gas burst out, taking shape, revealing an unmistakable silhouette of their scaly visitor. Agent Mamba lowered his gun, hitting a red button on the side of it and aiming it once again—firing! A red bullet shot out of the chamber, traveling towards Partitus. Exploding milliseconds before impact, leaving a wet red blob on his shoulder.

All you could see was the red blob floating away from them.

AGENT FD LANCE

"Continue to pursue after him! I will go around and cut him off; this alley only turns left after a while. I'll have the device waiting to trap him!"

Agent FD Lance ran towards the car and opened the door.

AGENT MAMBA

"Lance!"

She looked up and stared at her partner.

AGENT MAMBA

"Please, be careful!"

She jumped inside the car, reversed quickly, and peeled off forward even faster. Agent Mamba watched her turn the corner before running after Partitus.

Agent FD Lance arrived at the other side of the alley, not seeing anyone in sight yet. She parked and got out. Lance tossed the duffle bag to the ground, dropping to one knee, and unzipped it. She reached in and took out the humming device.

She took a couple of deep breaths.

AGENT FD LANCE

"Okay! Do just like the manual said. This button, this binary pattern, and we should be—."

PARTITUS
"—golden??"

Agent FD Lance quickly jumped to her feet, turning to aim her gun at Partitus, who was uncamouflaged behind her. He slapped the gun out of her right hand and grabbed her throat, raising her off the ground where she couldn't breathe. The device began to flash and light up in her opposite hand.

PARTITUS
"Where did you get the technology
to make this device??"

Partitus yanked it from her, examining it before tossing it over his shoulder. Then, with some strength, Agent FD Lance opened her mouth to speak.

AGENT FD LANCE
"What do you want from us??"

Partitus smiled.

PARTITUS
"—to cause confusion, chaos, jealously—<u>DIVISION</u>!"

He pulled her closer to him until they were face-to-face.

PARTITUS
"Does _THAT_ answer your question
— niña huérfana??"

Behind them, the device became fully activated, illuminating the alley with a blue flashing light. As the blue orb expanded, filling the center where shades of blue and yellow lighting lashed out.

Partitus looked back.

Agent FD Lance jabbed him in his throat with the rest of her strength. He let go of hers as he grabbed at his. His gills opened and closed repeatedly. Finally, she dropped, hitting the concrete, where she gasped for air. The device began to rattle, from a peaceful humming sound to a full-blown thunderstorm with vacuum-like sucking winds. Partitus was slowly being sucked in towards the machine. As the lightning made its way around his body, pulling him.

But it wasn't enough!

Agent FD Lance stood up slowly, staring at him, watching him struggle.

She backed up.
She charged towards him.

She began to gather speed along the way!

She approached Partitus, ran up his body, and performed a backflip, pushing off his chest and sending him backward. But his tail wrapped around one of her ankles in the middle of her backflip. She was yanked out of the sky backward as he stumbled, stepping on the device. He immediately began to sink inside the vast blue center, where the orb fully expanded.

Agent FD Lance connected with the concrete again, hitting her head and back hard. She became super dizzy as the environment around her spun.

While still being dragged right along with him into the device!

PARTITUS
"If I go, you go with me!"

AGENT MAMBA
"Nu-uh! Not today!"

An all-black katana blade came slicing down through the powerful winds. Cutting through Partitus's thick tail, blood splattered everywhere.

He screamed in pain.

PARTITUS

"I will take everything from you! Do you hear me?? Piece by piece until you have nothing left! <u>NOTHING LEFT!!!</u>"

Both agents walked up to Partitus, whose head was only now left to be swallowed.

AGENT FD LANCE

"You can't curse me. I've been anointed by the Highest."

PARTITUS

"This I can see. But no. Not you, I can't. But through your sin, I can!"

Agent FD Lance continued staring as Partitus drowned in the blue orb as she touched her stomach.

Partitus nodded with a smile on his face.

PARTITUS

"I'll be back for the final piece niña huérfana."

They could hear his evil laugh as the rest of Partitus vanished inside the device.

Both agents were met at the agency with an erupt of applause. Everyone was on their feet clapping, patting them on their backs as they walked past, congratulating them. Agent FD Lance sharply turned and grabbed one of the people who slapped her back by the shirt.

AGENT MAMBA
"Oh! You shouldn't have done that! She
said she banged her back up bad!"

DIRECTOR
"Agent, let him go, please. And follow me. Agent
Mamba, good job; go hit the showers and rest."

AGENT MAMBA
"Yes Ma'am."

Agent FD Lance followed the Director into a
conference room nearby. Everyone was looking at
them through the windows of the room. Then the
windows all darkened and disappeared, becoming
what looked like an ordinary wall.

Agent Mamba walked away.

DIRECTOR
"So, how long would you keep this
a secret from me??"

AGENT FD LANCE
"What are you talking about??"

DIRECTOR
"Don't fool with me, Lance! I will drop you back off
where I found you. Mind wiped and everything!"

DOCTOR TAMAH
"That won't be necessary, Director. Let's
all calm down and relax. Breath. Okay??
Good! Now Agent Lance—."

AGENT FD LANCE
"—FD Lance, doctor!"

DOCTOR TAMAH
"Right! Sorry. (clears throat) FD Lance, as you
know, there are technologies in the suits.
Designed to check your vitals and ensure
everyone is okay throughout your missions.
I would like to believe that you would have
known we would have found out."

AGENT FD LANCE
"—And??"

DIRECTOR
"And?? Little girl, do you know that you
are three months pregnant?? I saw that
little Bruce Lee stunt you did!"

AGENT FD LANCE
"Yes! And everything will be okay. I don't even
know if I'm going to keep it. You guys need
me here working for the agency. Plus, I can't
have him anyway. So why keep the baby?"

DIRECTOR
"Lance, don't contribute to something you will
deeply regret later. Trust me; you don't want
to go down that path. No occupation is worth
having a beautiful thing. So I am putting you on
temporary leave. Sleeper status. Two years max."

AGENT FD LANCE
"What?? No! I need to work! How
am I going to survive?"

DIRECTOR
"Don't worry; you work for the government;
we have amazing benefits. You'll still be
getting your full pay. Now—goodbye."

Agent FD Lance opened the conference door coming
face-to-face with Agent Mamba.

He looked confused and worried.

AGENT MAMBA
"Are you—"

She pushed past him leaving him with his half-
asked sentence.

AGENT MAMBA
"Okay?"

DIRECTOR

"Agent Mamba, I know you would hit the showers and get some rest. But I wanted to tell you because Agent FD Lance is your partner. As of immediately, she is going into sleeper mode."

AGENT MAMBA
"What?? No! Can I know why??"

DIRECTOR
"That's not my place to tell you. Agent Lance will not have her mind wiped; she will take some personal time. To handle some personal things."

AGENT MAMBA
"May I ask for how long?"

DIRECTOR
"Two years, max."

AGENT MAMBA
"Then I am taking two years! I am not going that long without my partner. Plus, I need to spend more time with my family anyway."

DIRECTOR
"I figured that was coming. Very well, two years max sleeper mode granted. But before this takes place, I have one more mission for you. You'll be accompanying Doctor Tamah on this one. We need to figure more out on this Partitus creature."

AGENT MAMBA
"Yes ma'am."

DIRECTOR
"Good. The briefing will be first thing tomorrow."

TWO YEARS LATER...

CHAPTER III

THE DOCTOR'S OFFICE, PART 1

David stood in the bathroom, looking at himself in the half-steamy mirror.

Fresh out of the shower, he wore a towel wrapped around his waist. Water was still making its way down his chocolate skin, starting from his broad shoulders and traveling down his muscular chest and back. He flexed, causing every muscle to bulge as he nodded, grinning.

Then there was movement coming from outside the bathroom door. David looked over at the door, then glanced back at his reflection. He relaxed his body as his arms dropped to his side, and an overwhelming sadness came over him.

All he could think about—was her.

WIFE
"David? Is everything okay in there?"

DAVID
"—Uh, YES, honey, dear! Just got
finished washing up."

David briefly turned off the bathroom lights and stared at the mirror before leaving.

WIFE
"Good morning, my handsome king!"

David smiled.

DAVID
"Good morning, my beautiful queen!"

He walked over to a big comfy bed where his wife was lying and kissed her.

WIFE
"Last night was amazing!"

DAVID
"When is it not??"

WIFE
"—Well, there was that one time!"

David rolled his eyes, and his wife began to laugh teasingly.

DAVID

"Oh boy, here we go. Are you talking
about when I had a cold??"

WIFE
"Oh! So, it was a common cold, huh?? Hmm—."

DAVID
"Woman, stop playing with me! You know I put
up MJ numbers even when I'm sick. Especially
when I had you like Niagara Falls!"

His wife rolled her eyes, shaking her head and
laughing.

WIFE
"I swear you're too much! But I love
it, though. I love you."

He leaned over and gave her another kiss.

DAVID
"And I love you."

She smiled, blushing.

DAVID
"I'm heading downstairs to make breakfast. Do you
want something before we have to head out?"

A worrying look came across her face as she sat up in
their bed.

WIFE
"I don't know; I'm super nervous."

David looked at his wife sympathetically and sat on the bed next to her.

DAVID
"I know, baby. I am too. Whatever happens, whatever the results may be. We get through it together."

She looked at her husband and forced a smile nodding her head. Then, she leaned in towards her husband, and he gave her a peck on her forehead.

Downstairs, David cooked breakfast, and they ate quickly.

Shortly after, they both got dressed and headed outside to the car. He opened the door and helped his wife climb into their vehicle. Once inside himself, he started it and proceeded to back out. He looked over at his nervous wife. She glanced back at him and gave a half-smile, prompting him to put the SUV back into park. He reached over the middle console, grabbed her hand, and looked into her eyes.

DAVID
"We're in this together, okay, babe?"

WIFE

"I know, honey; I want this day to be over already."

David nodded understanding and kissed her hand, trying to provide some comfort.

It was a quiet drive for most of the way.

David wanted to say something, but what would it have been? What else could he have said that he hasn't said already? David loved his wife and would do anything to protect her. But this was something different, something he nor any other man could defeat or save their significant other from, especially when it could happen to anyone. And you wouldn't even see it coming! David was sad on the inside. He couldn't even imagine how his wife must have felt. She had always wanted this for them for a very long time!

They began seeing fewer community-gated homes and more corporate workers and buildings. Both men and women were in business suits, with gelled-back hairdos, and wearing shiny and expensive jewelry. On their cell phones buzzing around on autopilot like worker bees, ignoring and walking past the men and women in dirty, ripped-up clothes. Who had dirt smeared all over their faces and mingling with their messy hair. The homeless were scattered everywhere! Some were sleeping on park benches; some huddled together with given-up faces, and others were hunting for food in dumpsters.

David was pulling up to a yellow traffic light when he saw a woman who got shoved out of a parked tinted window car. She stumbled and found herself falling forward. Face planting, hitting the concrete hard on the sidewalk. She looked back with a scowl as money was thrown at her, which the woman hurried and scurried to pick up. She shoved the money in her dingy bra behind her ripped-up shirt.

Whoever she was, her face was covered in dirt, bruises, and scratches. Her hair was mangled and all over the place, and so was her lipstick. She stood up and pulled up her wrinkled and spot-stained pants, buttoning them. She continued to give whoever was in the car a mean stare.

PERSON IN CAR
"I'll see you in a couple of days, trash."

The car door was slammed shut as it burnt rubber driving off, almost swiping David's car as it cut them off. David slammed his fist down on the horn, but the car was already too far to even care. David sat back and looked at his wife, who was looking at the woman.

She scoffed.

WIFE
"See that there! That is what's slowing down women's progress. No respect. Just disgusting!"

DAVID
"Babe?"

David rolled his eyes and shook his head as they drove off once the light turned green. David was not trying to add more stress and craziness to what they already had going in their lives.

Once at their family doctor's office, they sat holding hands when the doctor came in. She closed the door behind her as she forced a weak smile. Sadness and unfortunate news were written all over her face. She looked down at the paperwork on her clipboard and looked back, disappointedly shaking her head.

DOCTOR
"I am sorry, Michelle. I truly am."

The doctor left room as Michelle collapsed into her husband's arms, face buried in his chest where she cried uncontrollably.

Tears also ran down David's face, standing there trying to keep himself together enough to comfort his wife.

He kissed her forehead before resting his wet cheek

on it.

DAVID

"I am so sorry, baby. But we will get through this! We will find another solution, another way—we always do!"

CHAPTER IV

THE SILVER LINING!

Michelle sat on her side of the bed as she stared towards the window. A little bit of sunlight snuck its way through the cracks of the closed bamboo shades.

DAVID

"Michelle. You're barely eating anything. It's been several months since you left this room."

MICHELLE

"What's the point of eating anything at all? It's not like there's a reason to put food in my stomach."

David rolled his eyes, shaking his head.

DAVID

"Well, how about so you don't starve to death, huh?? When was the last time you took a shower? A bath?? And this room! It's a mess! And you—."

Michelle sharply turned her neck and head and gave

David an even sharper stare.

MICHELLE
"—And I what, David??"

DAVID
"Baby. I love you with <u>ALL</u> my heart! With everything I have! But! Look at you. You haven't had a decent sleep. Hence the bags under your eyes. Even when you're awake, you haven't left the bed."

MICHELLE
"David! My life is in shambles right now! A piece of my life was ripped away from me! No. The very reason for me even breathing has been stolen from me! So, I'm sorry I haven't been a full-fledged catwalk model for you since we left the hospital."

DAVID
"Babe…I'm sorry, I didn't—."

Tears began to form in her eyes.

DAVID
"Let's…let's do something tonight. Let's go out. Get something to eat. You know, get some fresh air?"

Michelle, with tears running down her face, looked at David.

She nodded.

David smiled.

DAVID

"How about this? I have to stop by the
office to meet with my boss still. So you
get cleaned up and put on that dress I like.
And I'll be back to pick you up. Okay?"

MICHELLE

"—Can we have sushi?"

David laughed.

DAVID

"Yes. We can have sushi."

* * * * *

Michelle and David were sitting at a table in the back
of a fancy sushi restaurant. David sat back in his
chair, watching his wife stuff her face with raw fish.
He covered his mouth, trying to hide his laughter.
She looked up at him with chopsticks full of sushi
halfway to her mouth. They stared at one another.
The sushi began to slip between the chopsticks and
then dropped back onto her plate. Causing dipping
sauce to splash everywhere. She looked down at her
plate and back up at David with a shocked face.

This time, they both covered their mouths,
laughing.

DAVID
"That good, huh??"

MICHELLE
"Mmm…yes! Try some David!"

DAVID
"Now you know I don't touch that stuff!
Unless it's fried in some type of oil!"

Michelle rolled her eyes, giggling.

David chuckled. Then with a smile left on his face, he stared at her with dreamy eyes.

She blushed.

MICHELLE
"What?"

DAVID
"I'm glad I finally got you out of that room. And you look gorgeous tonight—like you do—every time."

Michelle's eyes began to water. Both tears and mascara began to make their way down her cheeks. David quickly grabbed his clothed napkin and dipped it in his cup of water. Then, he leaned over to wipe his wife's face.

DAVID
"Oh, baby, I'm sorry, I didn't mean to—."

Michelle grabbed his hand as her husband touched her cheek with the damp napkin.

MICHELLE
"Honey, it's okay. I'm okay. It's just; I want to say— thank you. Thank you for not giving up on me."

David smiled.

DAVID
"On us, I haven't given upon us. And that reminds me. I have some exciting news."

Michelle's face lit up with excitement.

David reached into his jacket pocket and handed her a folded-up piece of paper. He watched as his wife unfolded the paper and began to read whatever was on it. Then, without warning, she covered her mouth and burst into tears. She looked up at David, nodding her head.

DAVID
"Is that a yes?"

Michelle, still crying, nodded even harder!

DAVID

"I'm sorry, what was that?? I can't make out what you're saying. I'm hard of hearing."

David got up and kneeled next to Michelle, grabbing her hand. He looked up at her, smiling. With even more tears and mascara running down her cheeks, laughing, Michelle nodded even harder.

MICHELLE
"YES! Yes, thousand times over, yes!
How did this happen?? I mean, when??
Isn't there some process??"

DAVID
"It's all been handled by my job. That's why
my boss wanted me to swing by. She told me
it would be doing her a huge favor and mean
the world to her if I did this. She said—it
would be my greatest and last job for her."

MICHELLE
"So…when do we—?"

DAVID
"—tomorrow."

*   *   *   *   *

Michelle sat in the passenger seat the following day, squirming, excited and nervous. David glanced over and smiled.

DAVID
"You'll be great, baby. Everything
will be fine; try to relax."

She nodded as she bit her nails and glanced out the car window.

The ride seemed to take forever as so many thoughts ran through her mind. But the mini road trip ended with them driving through an already-opened iron gate. Finally, David pulled into a driveway of a big ranched-style house with a well-kept yard. David parked and proceeded to turn the car off.

He grabbed the key, and before twisting it, he looked at his wife again. She looked back at him nervously. Then she nodded. He turned off the car, and they got out.

The front door opened, and David's boss stood in the doorway.

DAVID
"Director—."

DIRECTOR
"David—."

The Director smiled sadly as she led them into the house, stopping at the living room where the Director's husband stood.

He had tears in his eyes as he made eye contact with David. They both nodded. The Director's husband looked down to his side. Behind him, gripping his legs, was a little girl peeking through them. He guided her around from behind him into the open. Michelle's eyes got wide as they watered, and her instantly falling in love. The little girl's thick, curly black hair flowed over her pink overalls. You could tell that she was curious as her bushy eyebrows moved up and down. While her dark brown almond eyes darted up and down, examining Michelle. She was an unbelievably beautiful little girl with flawless sandy brown skin. She looked to be maybe four or five years old.

The Director approached the little girl, who raised her arms to be picked up. The Director smiled and picked her up, planting a big kiss on the little girl's cheek. Her husband planted another on the opposite cheek. The little girl bunched up, laughing at the kisses tickling her. Then the little girl looked at the Director and pointed at David and Michelle.

DIRECTOR
"Ruth, say hello to your new mommy
and daddy, okay?"

Ruth grabbed the handle of her pacifier and took it out of her mouth.

RUTH
"My daddy?"

CHAPTER V

THE DOCTOR'S OFFICE, PART 2

Over the following several months, David and Michelle spent much time with Ruth.

Trying to get to know who this little girl was, doing their best to make her feel at home and part of a family. At first, she'd stay up crying, walking around with her blanket looking for the Director and her husband. Michelle would then carry her back to her little bed and sleep with her. Then she would wake up and see Ruth cuddled up and sound asleep, with David in their room.

Eventually, that's who she wanted, David.

And no one else.

DAVID
"Go find your coat so we can go bye-
bye, okay, honey?"

RUTH

"Okay, daddy."

Ruth turned and began to skip and sing down the hall to her room. Then there was a flush in the master bathroom, and Michelle came out.

DAVID
"You almost ready to go? You know the doctors hate waiting on us."

MICHELLE
"Yes, David, I am almost ready. And I don't need you checking up on me. Do that with *your* daughter, not me. Since you guys are *so buddy, buddy.*"

DAVID
"You know, it's *so* funny how doctors will CHARGE you a cancelation or late fee. But be 24 hours late to the appointment when we arrive on time! How is that fair? Wait—What? *My* daughter?? Excuse me??"

MICHELLE
"You know she hasn't called me mommy yet?? Hell! She doesn't even let me hold her! All she wants is you! I'm her mommy David! SHE SHOULD LOVE ME!!"

David leaned back to peer out past the door into the hallway. He could still hear Ruth singing and moving around in her bedroom.

DAVID

"Lower your voice for one! Second, you need to give her time. It's only been months. In her defense, I've had more time with her than you."

MICHELLE

"What does that mean, David??"

DAVID

"Well…when we left the hospital, you were so stressed and sad. It weighed down on me; I needed to talk to someone. And I went to the Director, and I confided in her. She was hesitant, but she told me about Ruth. She has been taking care of her ever since she was a baby. Now, they're getting older and can't chase after her like they used to. She asked if we could take her in because our situation called for it. I said yes, and—they got to work on the papers immediately. Through all that time, I would stop by here 'n' there to spend time with her."

MICHELLE

"Wow. So funny."

DAVID

"—What is?"

MICHELLE

"Nothing. It's (scoffing)—whatever."

Michelle grabbed her fur coat off the bed and placed

It across her arm. She turned her back on David as she headed to the door. David rushed past her and pushed the door shut.

Ruth jumped inside her room from the slam as she looked towards her door into the hallway.

DAVID
"What! Is. Funny??"

MICHELLE
"Move, David!"

DAVID
"Not until you tell me what's so funny about trying to put the pieces of my wife back together??"

Michelle laughed, stepping backward.

MICHELLE
"You, David! You're funny! Do you know why and how?? You're always trying to control everything and…and calling it fixing something! You went behind my back to set up an 'I got the hookup' adoption without telling me about it! Why?? Because you felt like you needed to fix your wife's life because she was, how'd you say it?? Oh! In pieces??"

DAVID
"That's not fair, Michelle! I did this for us—for you!"

MICHELLE
"I'M THE ONE WHO CAN'T HAVE A
BABY, DAVID! NOT YOU! Not you. You
never gave me a chance to—."

DAVID
"So why did you say yes then?"

MICHELLE
"I was vulnerable, David. And I needed it! I
wanted this so badly. A baby was something
I would never be able to have. So, without
overthinking it. I said yes. I want to love her;
I do. I'm trying! But how? When you <u>FINALLY</u>
get the one thing you <u>ALWAYS</u> wanted. And you
love it! To find out the love isn't mutual?"

DAVID
"Is that what this is <u>ALL</u> about?? Because I barely
got a jumpstart being in our daughter's life??"

Michelle stared at David blankly. David scoffed out
loud.

DAVID
"I'm sure it's safe to say we wouldn't be having this
conversation if she warmed up to you right out the
gates, huh? So you say you're trying to love her?"

MICHELLE

"Yes! With <u>ALL</u> my heart David!"

DAVID
"Then give her some time. Continue to be the good mom I know you can be. And give her time."

RUTH
"Daddy?"

Michelle rolled her eyes.

DAVID
"Can we go?? We're going to be late! And I'm going to be charged a late fee!"

Finally, with everybody inside the car, driving and surrounded by familiar buildings, business people, and homeless folk. David was approaching a yellow light. He slowed down and stopped as the light turned red. David looked over at his wife, who had her face buried in her phone. He shook his head and looked in the backseat. Ruth was sleeping.

As the stoplight turned green and David took his foot off the brakes to go. A tinted window car swerved in front of them, cutting them off as it turned the corner. David hit the brakes hard again! Michelle was jerked forward as her phone fell to the floor. David immediately looked in the back seat. Ruth moved a little bit but stayed asleep.

DAVID
"Is that the same—?"

MICHELLE
"I think so—."

DAVID
"Okay, hold on."

MICHELLE
"—David??"

David hit the gas pedal and swerved around the corner in pursuit of the reckless driver.

MICHELLE
"David, can you <u>PLEASE LET IT GO</u>??
Ruth has a checkup in less than 15
minutes. Rember the late fee!"

DAVID
"Oh, don't worry, babe, I'm about to
charge it to this ass whooping!"

David sped up.

Once they caught up to the car, it was parked outside an alleyway. David pulled up behind it and parked. He looked over at Michelle and then back at Ruth.

DAVID

"Stay in the car and keep the car running."

Then he got out.

MICHELLE
"—David??"

David walked up slowly to the car and tapped on the window.

No one replied.

He grabbed the door handle and tugged, cracking open the door. Then he heard a female scream. David looked up towards the alley.

WOMAN
"LET ME GO!!!"

David quickly but quietly rushed to the opening of the alley. His body was pressed against the wall as he peeked. There were three big guys and one small female. They had her backed up against a wall. Two pinned her down as the third slapped her hard across her face, followed by a backhand.

THIRD GUY
"Listen here—trash! The boss is expecting you! He wants his money _AND_ his weekly dose of his favorite sugar! Because it will be your fault that we're late in the first place. The

guys and I will take our cut of the sugar right <u>NOW</u>! I mean, hell, you're everyone's favorite anyway! Will the boss even notice?"

They all laughed except the woman, who was now bleeding from a cut across the bridge of her nose. She stared at the third guy with anger in her eyes.

THIRD GUY
"Aww…Look, boys! Someone didn't think my joke was funny."

He walked closer to her.

David could hear him unzipping his pants.

THIRD GUY
"If I can be honest with you. You're not going to like the next three either."

The woman spat in his face.

He smacked her again.

She flung face first, flopping into the brick wall where the two guys grabbed her once more.

THIRD GUY
"Ya, perfect. Leave the trash just like that."

He got closer and let his pants fall to his ankles,

revealing his boxers with a bulge in the front. He reached out and grabbed the lady's waist pulling her towards him. As he did, her leg shot backward, connecting between the pervert's legs as he hunched over in pain. His face was met with another kick, sending him unconscious to the ground.

The other two guys looked down at their fallen comrade and then at the woman. The one on her right pulled his fist back, ready to hit her. The other guy on her left grabbed her even tighter as she struggled to escape.

Seeing that she wouldn't get free, she closed her eyes.

DAVID
"Nu-uh! Not today!"

The guy's arm was cut off in mid-swing by David's arm as their arms locked. Then he was flipped over David's hip, hitting the ground hard, where David landed a blow on his chin. He went unconscious immediately!

The last guy, still holding onto the woman, pulled her closer to him. He was backing away from David, who was walking closer to them. Then, without warning, the woman stomped on her capturer's foot. He let go of her, and as he did, she flipped forward, leaving her feet. Then, in the air, both of the woman's feet, one after the other, connected with his chin. And the impact sent him backward, crumbling to the floor, where she landed before David.

David took a step back as they stood there staring at one another.

He couldn't believe it!

Her thick and juicy lips were dry, cracked, and bleeding. Her once shiny and fruity-smelling hair was now mangled and dirty. Her small button nose had a deep gash across it. Her eyebrows were now bushily resting above her almond-shaped eyes, which had dark rings underneath them.

Blotched makeup, dirt, and bruises caked her face, swelling it to where you couldn't see her high cheekbones. She smelled of body odor as more dirt, scabs, cuts, and scrapes were scattered across her 'coconut shell' brown-colored skin.

DAVID

"Rebeka?? Wha…what have they done to you??"

She stared at David blankly.

REBEKA

"—Do I know you?"

DAVID
"Yes! Yes, you do! Or you should. Do you
not recognize me?? Do you not remember
who I am? Or who I was to you?"

She shook her head, now looking confused.

David looked at the guys on the ground as they woke
up. He grabbed her hand and began to turn to run
away. Rebeka withdrew her hand quickly and stared
at him with scared but focused eyes. David stepped
closer to Rebeka. She stepped backward. David
stopped and looked down at the ground closing his
eyes.

DAVID
"I am so sorry that they did this to you. I
should have stayed close to you, Rebeka.
This stuff wouldn't have happened."

David looked up at her with tears in his eyes.

DAVID
"You have no reason to trust me or <u>ANYONE</u>,
especially after looking like you've been
through hell. Let me show you I am only
trying to help. Let me prove to you I am a
friendly. We can get you something to eat. Get
you cleaned up. When was the last time you
took a warm bath? Slept on a soft bed??"

Rebeka stared at David and then looked down at her attackers.

She then looked back up at David and nodded her head slowly.

He smiled, took his jacket, and wrapped it around her, guiding her out of the alley.

Michelle, full of anxiety, back at the car, watched as David and a stranger approached. He opened the back door opposite where Ruth was sitting.

MICHELLE
"Thank God you are okay! You had me so worried!" David got into the driver's seat, where Michelle overwhelmed him with hugs and kisses.

DAVID
"I'm okay. Everything is fine, babe. But
we need to get out of here <u>ASAP</u>! And oh,
this is Rebeka. She needs our help."

Michelle looked at Rebeka in the backseat with a disguised look on her face.

MICHELLE
"No! Hell no! Why is this filthy prostitute
in the backseat of our car?? And next to our
daughter—which we had to reschedule her
doctor's appointment, by the way!"

Rebeka, from the backseat, stuck up her middle finger at Michelle. Then, she turned to get out of the car, which failed due to the child lock.

DAVID
"MICHELLE! Please?? Rebeka, don't do that, please?? Our daughter's back there, and I need you women to trust me on this!"

Michelle was staring at her husband with anger all over her face!

MICHELLE
"First chance we get, I want an explanation ASAP! Then, I want a Taylor-Burton type of diamond—on my finger immediately!"

David looked at his wife as she talked ridiculously.

MICHELLE
"—or something close to it, damn it!"

David nodded his head in agreement as he shifted the car into drive. The SUV's tires spun rapidly as they burnt rubber, leaving tire marks and smoke behind as they sped off!

RUTH
"Mommy—?"

Michelle looked at David, smiling. Then Michelle looked back at Ruth with tears in her eyes.

MICHELLE
"Yes, sweetie?"

Ruth stared back at Michelle, smiling.

RUTH
"Mommy!"

MICHELLE
"Yup! I'm your mommy! And mommy loves you!"

Michelle turned back around in her seat with a huge smile.

MICHELLE
"Oh my God, David! Can you believe it??
She finally said, mommy! Wow! You know
what? You were right. Time! She just needed
some time. I am so excited right now!"

David looked in the rearview mirror at Ruth while Michelle was talking. He watched as she reached over and grabbed Rebeka's hand. Rebeka jumped as she was startled by Ruth's touch.

Full of anxiety and confusion, Rebeka looked down at Ruth, who was smiling and pointing at her.

RUTH
"Mommy!"

CHAPTER VI
MESSY

DAVID

"You told me she was on sleep status! You never told me you wiped your mind and fed her to the wolves! How cold are you??"

David stood in the office facing his Director. Dr. Tamah was sitting at a computer nearby. She was on her way to stand up when the Director placed her hand on her shoulder.

DOCTOR TAMAH

"I was going to give you guys some privacy."

DIRECTOR

"You're fine. No privacy is needed because I don't know what David is talking about."

DAVID

"REBEKA, Director! I'm talking about Rebeka."

The Director's face went pale.

DIRECTOR
"She's alive??"

David's eyes narrowed as he studied his Director.

DAVID
"You…didn't know??"

The Director shook her head slowly, reaching for a chair, which Dr. Tamah helped her sit down.

DIRECTOR
"Thank you, dear. But, I swear, I didn't, David, especially with a wiped mind."

DAVID
"Then who has the power within STAR to order a memory wipe beside you?"

The Director looked up at David with wide eyes.

DIRECTOR
"—Only me!"

David walked closer to his boss with anger on his face.

DIRECTOR
"David…calm down."

Yet, he drew closer.

DOCTOR TAMAH
"David, please, you're acting irrationally! Stop!"

David stood before the Director and grabbed her by her shirt collar—lifting her off the chair. He brought her face closer to his baring his teeth. Then immediately, he dropped her as he buckled, hitting the ground. The Director fell backward, holding a remote in her hand. She stood up and straightened her clothes. She then kneeled beside David as he grunted in pain, holding his chest.

DIRECTOR
"Don't you <u>EVER</u> put your hands on me, little boy! I care for you like a son, but I will burst your heart open like I <u>NEVER</u> met you! Now listen to me!"

The Director hit a button on the remote in her hand, and the pain subsided. David was on the floor, panting heavily. He looked up at the Director.

DAVID
"You…made your…point. Now explain…please."

DIRECTOR
"The last time I saw Rebeka was a little after she gave birth. Five months to be exact. She dropped Ruth off and told us she would return soon. But she never came back. I tried <u>EVERYTHING</u> in my power to find my baby! She was AWOL."

David grabbed the table, pulled himself up to a nearby chair, and sat in it.

DAVID
"Wait, wait, wait. Backup. Ruth's her daughter??"

DIRECTOR
"Not only hers."

DOCTOR TAMAH
"What do you mean, Director??"

DIRECTOR
"It's their daughter. David and Rebeka's daughter."

Both anger and jealousy swept across Doctor Tamah's face. She stood up, excusing herself as she exited the room hurriedly.

DIRECTOR
"Where is my daughter now, David?"

DAVID
"At my home with Ruth…and Michelle."

The Director walked past David shaking her head, and walking out of the office.

DIRECTOR
"Messy. Now take me to my daughter
and my grandbaby."

DAVID
"Yes, ma'am."

David followed the Director out of the office where Doctor Tamah was waiting. David stopped dead in his tracks, seeing her stomach. It was huge! He looked at her; then he looked over at the Director. She shook her head once again before walking off.

DIRECTOR
"Like I said…messy."

DOCTOR TAMAH
"Can we talk, please?"

CHAPTER VII
"—IN THIS LIFE OR THE NEXT—."

Doctor Tamah came rushing to her office, located inside the sea lab. She quickly slammed the door behind her, collapsed on the floor, and sobbed!

DOCTOR TAMAH
"It <u>IS HIS</u>! Why would he deny it?? I don't understand. He's the only <u>man</u> I've ever been with intimately! Is there something wrong with me?? If so, what is it??"

Doctor Tamah dropped to the floor and continued to sob.

PARTITUS
"Nothing is wrong with you, beautiful! You are perfect!"

Doctor Tamah stopped crying.

DOCTOR TAMAH
"What do you want?? Leave me alone!"

PARTITUS

*"Ahh…quid tibi est, puella pulchra? Especially
with all of the time we spent together?
<u>Things</u>—we have done together."*

DOCTOR TAMAH

"Shut up! Why are you talking to me??"

PARTITUS

"Cur tam pulchra facies lacrimas habet??"

Doctor Tamah looked at her reflection on the shiny
floor. And saw only tears and a hopeless face.

DOCTOR TAMAH

"He denied me. He's denied <u>OUR</u> son! He denied <u>US</u>!"

PARTITUS

"Why do you think that is? How do you know it's his?"

DOCTOR TAMAH

"What do you mean?? I'm not some slut!"

PARTITUS

"Oh no, of course not—."

DOCTOR TAMAH

"The first time…it shouldn't have happened. The
mission should have been strictly professional.
But the atmosphere, the scenery, was so romantic!

And David was just always so charming and so—good looking. I felt safe around him and wanted to be in his muscular arms, resting my head on his chest as we gazed into one another's eyes! Oh! I was so dumb! Inexperienced, vulnerable, and gullible. I would have done anything to please David. BUT NOW LOOK AT ME??"

She continued to cry.

PARTITUS

*"I've been around for an exceedingly long time. I've grown to know men. To know that they are easily distracted. They **BECOME** easily distracted. As easy as seeing a woman bathing from the rooftops. And before you know it, you have her impregnated and her husband killed in battle. The question is, why? Why does this happen when men have so many women at their disposal? So. Many. Women. Hmm? As if one is never enough."*

DOCTOR TAMAH

"It's them! They are the problem! They are the distraction!"

PARTITUS

"Whatever do you mean, beautiful?"

DOCTOR TAMAH

"David. For one, he's married to that selfish witch Michelle! And second, he's so wrapped around

Rebeka's finger its—RIDICULOUS, DISGUSTING! IT HAS ALWAYS BEEN ABOUT HER! HE'S ALWAYS CHASING BEHIND HER LIKE SOME LOST PUPPY!"

PARTITUS
"Then she vanishes, leaves for years, leaving him! And who fills that void by taking care of him??"

DOCTOR TAMAH
"I DID!"

Tears began to roll down Doctor Tamah's cheeks.

PARTITUS
"Now, he's throwing you and your child away sicut vos guys non referre!"

DOCTOR TAMAH
"—he <u>IS</u>!"

PARTITUS
"And you know why you'll never matter??"

DOCTOR TAMAH
"—Because of Rebeka!"

PARTITUS
"Because of Rebeka."

She buried her face into her palms and began to cry uncontrollably.

DOCTOR TAMAH
"I don't know what to do!"

PARTITUS
"I do—!"

DOCTOR TAMAH
"Free you?"

PARTITUS
"Free me—."

Doctor Tamah climbed to her feet.

PARTITUS
"And I'll ensure you two are never far apart…in this life or the next…."

DOCTOR TAMAH
"What do you want in return?"

PARTITUS
"Besides my freedom? Nothing. I got what I already wanted. I'll handle it for you. Nobody will know—it'll be our little secret."

DOCTOR TAMAH
"You promise??"

PARTITUS

"I put that on my unborn child."

Doctor Tamah stood before Partitus, who had his hands crossed and a smile on his face. Between them was a wall of blue energy. She walked over to the wall and touched the bio scanner. It flashed green as the blue wall vanished. Partitus stared at Doctor Tamah with a grimace gaze as she hobbled over to him. Inside his cell was like a tank a pet turtle would have.

She stepped into the cell and walked up to Partitus.

DOCTOR TAMAH
"Now what??"

Partitus disappeared.

Doctor Tamah jumped back in fright. A pile of bones and a skull rested where Partitus was standing. She walked up to it and kneeled over the bones, examining them.

PARTITUS
"Pick me up and toss me into the water."

She did precisely that—standing at the edge, looking into the water. The surface began to bubble, and then Partitus emerged slowly. He looked like he did when he first was approached in the alley. He walked out of the water to Doctor Tamah, whose gaze never left him. He stood towering over her, looking down at her. He caressed her chin and cheek, causing her to blush and smile.

He closed his eyes, and his gills opened and closed deeply. Then he opened his eyes and stared back into Doctor Tamah's green eyes.

He wrapped his new tail around her body, pulling her into him—they kissed passionately.

Then without warning, Doctor Tamah pushed him away as she began to scream violently. She fell to the floor as she bit and clawed away at her clothes. Finally, the doctor lifted her shirt to see a bulge where the baby was, to see it moving around and pushing to get out!

An alarm immediately went off throughout the entire building.

Partitus smiled as he backed up, vanishing in thin air.

CHAPTER VIII
FINALLY, THE TRUTH—

DIRECTOR
"We have trouble inbound."

The Director walked into the living room, hanging up her phone. David stood in the center of the room while Michelle sat on the couch, staring at Ruth, standing next to Rebeka, holding her hand tightly.

DAVID
"What's wrong??"

DIRECTOR
"He's free, Partitus, you know…the self-important demon. And guess who freed him?"

David opened his mouth to answer.

DIRECTOR
"The baby momma that's <u>NOT</u> here. That's who. I'm assuming your conversation didn't go so well??"

DAVID
"—no."

DIRECTOR
"We need to be prepared to recapture the target. An evacuation team is on the way. Tag and bag that's the objective. Getting little Ruth, your wife, and concubine somewhere safe would be wise."

David took a deep breath and exhaled, giving the Director a straight face.

She gave one back.

DIRECTOR
"Is there a problem?"

David walked over to the couch where Michelle sat, staring into the distance. He kneeled in front of her placing his hands on her knees. She looked into his eyes, with tears rolling down her cheeks.

DAVID
"Baby?"

Michelle shook her head in disgust.

MICHELLE
"—don't!"

She looked over at Rebeka and Ruth.

MICHELLE
"That was never going to be my daughter…was it?"

David looked over his shoulder at Ruth, smiling at Rebeka. He smiled a sad smile and then looked down at the ground.

DAVID
"No. Ruth is Rebeka and my daughter."

Rebeka stared at David and then at Ruth with a confused look. The more she stared at Ruth, Rebeka could see herself—and David. This made her wonder, did she *really* have a life before surviving the streets?? Because obviously, she had people who cared about her.

David nodded his head slowly and stood up.

DAVID
"I just found out myself. I'm sorry."

MICHELLE
"David, that little girl is five. We have been married for almost ten years!"

DAVID
"—I'm sorry."

More and more tears came as Michelle stared at the

ceiling in disbelief.

MICHELLE
"When did this start happening?
And how many times?"

DAVID
"The first time was like any other time. A
couple of days before a mission."

MICHELLE
"Mission?? Recapture the target?? Why
are you guys talking like you're part of
some secret service or something??"

Both David and the Director stared at Michelle with
straight faces.

REBEKA
"I can hardly remember anything, and that's
the vibe I got from everyone here."

MICHELLE
"I thought you were an architect??"

David shook his head.

MICHELLE
"Wow. More lies. So, assuming you're telling
the truth, how many missions were there?
You know that you two had together?"

DIRECTOR
"Is this necessary right now?? In case you forgot, we have a killer demon on the way."

MICHELLE
"HOW MANY, DAVID??"

DAVID
"—A lot."

MICHELLE
"Every time you would <u>LEAVE TOWN FOR WORK</u>, you were just sleeping with this slut?? Right before you guys skip off, hold hands, and kill people?? Do I have it all down pretty accurately??"

DAVID
"We don't kill people; it's not that type of agency."

The Director shrugged her shoulders, balancing her hands in a "50/50" gesture.

MICHELLE
"Oh, but you <u>DO</u> sleep with sluts, though??"

REBEKA
"You know what, chica rubia?? I'm getting tired of you yelling! Also, the rude and cold stares at me like I'm stupid, calling me a puta! So you better watch your mouth before

I punch you in front of my daughter!"

MICHELLE
"Oh! I'm sorry! Now you remember
it's your daughter??"

Rebeka began to walk over to where Michelle was. Michelle jumped up from the couch and walked towards Rebeka. David stood in the center with his arms spread, trying to keep distance between them.

MICHELLE
"You need to choose David! Her or me??"

DIRECTOR
"ENOUGH!!! There is an ancient murderous
THING on its way here right now! We need
weapons in hand, and cooperation from
every adult here, assuming there are some
here. And somewhere safe for you three to
hide without tearing one another apart."

PARTITUS
"I would have let them keep arguing
if it was up to me."

Partitus came walking into the living room with a smirk on his face. Everyone backed up, trying to leave some space between them and him.

PARTITUS

"Is this how you treat your guess? If so, this is some bad hospitality. Tsk, tsk, tsk. No matter, I'm here to kill you all either way. Believe it or not, I like you, Michelle, but a promise is a promise."

REBEKA
"Who are you, and what do you want from us?"

PARTITUS
"You don't know why I'm here, Rebeka??"

REBEKA
"How do you know my name?"

PARTITUS
"Ohhh…I know a lot about you, *chica*! Every. Single. Thing. Your life is one of my favorite memoirs to read!"

REBEKA
"I…I don't understand."

PARTITUS
"What is there not to understand? I told you I was going to take everything away from you! Memory after memory until everyone you cared about and vice versa was unrecognizable."

DIRECTOR
"So, it was you who took her memory… through a curse, I assume? But how did

your curse get past the anointing??"

PARTITUS
"Director, I think we both know how. When the adults are away, the kids will play."

DIRECTOR
"—through her pregnancy. Through their sin."

PARTITUS
"Ding! Ding! Ding! Bingo! Now I'm here to take the last piece."

Partitus looked down at Ruth, who was gripping Rebeka's leg. And without warning, his tail whistled, cutting through the air at her! Inches away from Ruth, the Director jumped between her and Partitus's tail. As it shot through her shoulder, snatching her out of the air. Then tossing her to the side, where she hit the ground with a thud going unconscious.

PARTITUS
"The girl! Now!"

David stepped forward, standing in between the females and Partitus.

Partitus had a smirk on his face.

David didn't.

David balled his hands tightly to where his knuckles cracked and turned white.

DAVID
"Michelle, I want you to take everyone
to the safe room. Alright?"

Michelle's face turned from scared to angry as she stared at Rebeka.

Partitus's smirk grew wider.

CHAPTER IX

WHAT WAS ONCE LOST—

Michelle and Rebeka, holding Ruth, rushed inside the panic room. Where everything inside began to flicker and turn on.

Once fully inside, the bookshelf slid closed, leaving the study empty.

The panic room was filled with computers, security camera monitors, canned food, bottled water, and other essentials for survival. Then there was a wall, all by itself covered with every type of weapon imaginable. And in the center were two all-black katanas mounted parallel to one another.

REBEKA
"So…you never got a secret agent
vibe from all of this?"

Michelle shook her head slowly.

Rebeka sat Ruth down and walked to the security camera monitors, where Michelle joined her. They could see David and Partitus standing across from one another, measuring each other up, looking for weaknesses, and mentally planning out their plan of attack.

PARTITUS
"I never forgot how you cut off my tail, peasant.
For that, I will put you through a lot of pain.
And when I cripple you, I will make you
watch as I kill everyone in that room."

Partitus looked up at the camera hidden in the ceiling corner.

David reached behind his back and pulled out a sharp-looking blade that curved around his knuckles. He looked at Partitus and shook his head.

DAVID
"Nu-uh! Not today!"

Partitus rushed David as he leaned in with a left punch. David immediately ducked under his extended arm, cutting across his rib cage. Partitus yelled in pain as he quickly turned around, throwing a right jab toward David's head. David sidestepped out of the way and took to the air—returning a round kick connected with Partitus's jaw. That sent him to one knee as he held the cut wound across his ribs.

DAVID

"Stay down, Partitus!"

Partitus looked at his hand, covered in oozy green blood. He smiled, then chuckled to himself.

PARTITUS

"So, this is what it feels like to bleed? Interesting."

*   *   *   *   *

Michelle and Rebeka watched in fear when Rebeka grabbed her head. She screamed in pain and fell to her knees. Ruth ran over to her, hugging her as Michelle watched with horror and anxiety.

RUTH

"What is wrong, mommy??"

REBEKA

"I don't know, baby! I see images and thoughts about your Papi. Memories—I think I'm seeing memories of you and your Papi. I'm starting to remember."

Rebeka sat up, wiping tears from her eyes, and grabbed Ruth, hugging her tightly as Ruth giggled.

RUTH

"Mommy, your hair tickles!"

REBEKA

"I'm sorry, baby. I'm sorry it took so long to realize who you were to me and how special you are! And I've been absent from your life. But now, mommy must help your Papi beat the bad guy. Okay??"

At this point, Ruth had tears in her eyes as she looked her mom in the eyes. She smiled. Then grabbed her mom's face by the cheeks and gave her a peck on the lips.

RUTH

"Okay, mommy!"

Rebeka stood up and looked at Michelle. Michelle rolled her eyes.

MICHELLE

"Whatever. Sure. Go!"

Rebeka nodded and turned around, rushing over to the wall of weapons.

*   *   *

Partitus stood up and looked at David with a smirk on his face.

PARTITUS

"Maybe I underestimated your ability to battle David. You fight like a king I once knew. I will damage your pride with the honor your skillset deserves."

Partitus closed his eyes and stretched his arms wide as the house shook. David got into a defensive stance, unbothered by the house shaking—preparing himself for whatever was next. Then he heard a rushing coming from behind Partitus. David's eyes widened as powerful water jets on either side of Partitus shot toward him. He rolled to the side, dodging one blast with his blade still in hand.

He jumped to his feet but was met with a second blast of water. That took him off his feet, slamming him against one of the walls in the house. That crumbled and gave away, leaving a giant hole as he skitted across the dirt, landing a couple of feet away in his backyard!

David slowly got back up, covered in scrapes, cuts, and bruises, soaked in blood and water. He looked towards the house to see Partitus walking through the hole. Partitus was now wearing a gold helmet and dressed in matching gold armor that covered his entire body with spikes.

As he walked, a cape fluttered behind him as it moved in the night wind.

PARTITUS
"Ah, you're back on your feet, I see! You are strong, but not enough, I am afraid."

Before David could react or respond, Partitus was in front of him. He grabbed David's shirt and slammed him back to the ground punching him in the stomach. David buckled as he coughed up blood, dropping his blade. Partitus then hit him under his chin, sliding him backward, where Partitus appeared behind David. And picked him up by his wet and curly hair, slamming him face down into the ground a few times!

David rolled over, holding his stomach, groaning in pain, halfway unconscious.

But that didn't stop Partitus from crouching over him, repeatedly hitting him in the face.

Finally tired, Partitus grabbed David by the neck and lifted him. He turned David's head to the side and raised his other fist. His armor spread, covering his hand and forming a sharp jagged point.

PARTITUS
"I hope the Doctor doesn't mind having
you without working legs."

Partitus stretched his arm back, ready to bury the dagger into the back of David's neck. Until a figure wearing an all-black tactical suit. Came down from the sky doing a front flip bringing a black katana down on Partitus's arm. The blade had an icy blue smoky aura as it sliced through Partitus's armor like butter! Partitus screamed in pain, dropping David as his other arm was on the ground, splashing in a puddle of green blood.

Immediately to compensate for a lost arm, Partitus's golden armor covered his other hand with an even longer blade. Then, with swiftness and rage, he turned around and swiped at the figure in all black.

The swing was dodged, and Partitus was again met with a swing of the figure's blade. Cutting off the other arm as his pain echoed into the night sky. The figure in black, crouching in battle stance, sword held high, watched as Partitus screamed. And green blood spraying from his new wound.

The person dressed in black:

backed up,
charged towards Partitus,
picking up momentum along the way!

And approaching him, running up his body and performing a backflip—pushing off his chest. Sending him backward into the mud. Then landing in a crouching position gripping the sword's handle while its blade pierced into the ground for stability. The figure stood up, yanked the sword from the ground, and removed their helmets.

Rebeka ran to where David was lying on the ground, beaten up badly. Rebeka reached into her pocket and took out a syringe filled with a green liquid, which she stuck in his neck, and he began to heal rapidly.

David opened his eyes.

He saw Rebeka and quickly sat up.

REBEKA
"Whoa, Papi, take it easy. The serum will take a couple of minutes to do its job."

DAVID
"Thank you, because he was whooping my… wait, what did you just call me??"

Rebeka smiled.

REBEKA
"I *didn't* remember anything at first, but out of nowhere, I began to remember you…and our daughter. So, I'm back—and I'm here now!"

PARTITUS
"Oh, how touching! It doesn't matter what memories you get back! I am going to end you all, NOW!"

Rebeka helped David to his feet as they watched Partitus's armor shoot spikes from his backside into the ground, pushing himself up onto his feet. More spikes dug into the ground before him, helping him keep his balance. Rebeka reached behind her back, drew a second katana, and handed it to David. He smiled and grabbed the blade leaning in and kissing Rebeka. As they kissed, the same flexible black armor exceeded the katana's handle and covered his entire body.

REBEKA
"Let's go kick his ass!"

David nodded with a grin.

David and Rebeka raised their swords above their heads as they charged Partitus.

PARTITUS
"I'M GOING TO KILL YOU ALL, NOW!"

As they approached Partitus, spikes from his armor shot out at them. They dodged the shooting projectiles and, once close enough, took turns striking back, cutting through his armor.

Then Partitus began to change up his tactics to close-quarter combat. Causing Rebeka and David to block for one another as spikes shot out to impale! With every cut that left blood-leaking wounds on Partitus—Rebeka could feel more and more of her memories returning to her!

How she was raised by the Director and the Director's husband growing up.

SLASH!

She was bullied at grade school and finally fought back, sticking up for herself.

SLASH!

Her teenage years were she'd sneak out to go to parties.

SLASH!

She was at the top of her class when she graduated high school and college!

SLASH!

The Director, her mother, recruited and trained her to be an agent for the STAR. Where she met David in the academy for the first time—and their first mission together.

SLASH!

Rebeka and David's first time making love to one another and every time after that.

SLASH!

Later giving birth to their beautiful daughter Ruth.

SLASH!

She later had trouble remembering who David was or who Ruth was.

SLASH!

Tears poured down Rebeka's face as sadness, guilt, pain, and anger overwhelmed her.

SLASH!

She dropped Ruth off at the Director's house and drove away with everything going blank.

REBEKA
"YOU STOLE EVERYTHING FROM ME!"

David and Rebeka both brought down their swords cutting across Partitus's chest.

Green blood was splattered and scattered everywhere!

Partitus was covered in cuts all over his body as he kept himself up on one knee. David and Rebeka looked at each other and nodded. Then, they raised their swords, ready to strike once more! And as they did, two brand new arms shot out of the open wounds where Partitus's old arms were. He grabbed them both by the throat, squeezing. They dropped their katanas as they struggled to break free.

Partitus laughed, staring at them with tired yet determined eyes.

PARTITUS
"And I'm going to take more from you—<u>TRASH</u>!"

CLICK...BOOM!

David and Rebeka saw a surprised look sweep over Partitus's face. A hole appeared in his forehead where green blood began to leak out. His body dropped face first, letting them go as they fell to their knees, coughing and gasping for air. David looked to see a wobbly Director holding a smoking gun with blue liquid-filled bullets. She collapsed to the ground. The Director looked back up and stared at David and Rebeka with weary eyes. They got wider as she saw Rebeka rushing over to her, embracing The Director, kneeling and hugging her.

REBEKA

"I am so sorry, mama! I should have never left! I should have told you what I was going through. I didn't mean to forget you, I swear!"

The Director stared at her daughter with teary eyes and nodded. Rebeka continued to hug tightly as her mother kissed her forehead and patted the top of her crown.

Both cried with joy.

DIRECTOR
"Ouch! You gotta watch it, baby girl…
my arm got a hole in it now."

Rebeka looked at The Director apologetically, and they both laughed.

David walked over, joining them and helping his boss to her feet.

The Director then looked around, puzzled.

DIRECTOR
"WHERE IN THE HELL IS MY
EVACUATION TEAM??"

BRIEFING ENDED...

PROJECT
DAVID

CHAPTER X

HER?? OR ME, DAVID!

Michelle walked out of the study to the stair railing, holding Ruth. She looked down at David and Rebeka, who was helping The Director sit on one of the drier chairs. They all looked up at a scowling Michelle.

MICHELLE
"You need to choose! Her?? Or me, David??"

CHAPTER XI
HABITS DIE HARD

David stood in the bathroom, looking at himself again in the half-steamy mirror. He was wearing a robe shortly after getting out of the shower. When movement came from outside the bathroom door, he looked over at the door and then glanced back at his reflection.

All he could think about—was her.

WOMAN'S VOICE
"David? Is everything okay in there?"

DAVID
"…YES, honey, dear. Just got finished washing up."

David left the bathroom.

WOMAN'S VOICE
"Good morning, my handsome king!"

David smiled.

DAVID

"Good morning, my beautiful…wife."

He walked over to a big comfy bed where his wife was lying and kissed her.

CHAPTER XII

THE BIRTH OF SOMETHING NEW!

Alarms blared inside the agency as soldiers approached the lab room door.

They could only hear a woman's piercing scream inside—then dead silence.

The soldier quickly flooded the room with weapons drawn. They looked around and saw that the room was trashed. The lights were flickering on and off. Momentarily revealing claw marks scratched deeply into the walls and ceiling. The energy field that kept Partitus caged was turned off. And he was nowhere in sight!

CAPTAIN
"Lieutenant, I need you to get ahold of
The Director and tell her the prisoner
has escaped. Possibly inbound."

DOCTOR TAMAH
"It's already too late; he's going to be mine! He's
going to be with me always! This life—or the next."

CAPTAIN

"Doctor?? Is that you?? What transpired here?"

Doctor Tamah watched the soldiers from a dark corner of the room with red glowing eyes. Following every movement they made. The captain walked closer, slowly approaching where her voice came from. He reached on his ballistic vest and pulled off a flashlight.

He turned it on and aimed the high beam toward the corner. To only see the doctor launch toward him. Tackling him to the ground, clawing and tearing at the side of his neck, blood spraying everywhere.

When some got on her face, she lifted her head towards the ceiling and let out a high shriek as her mouth expanded—revealing razor-sharp teeth.

She hunched back over and dug her teeth into the captain's throat.

The rest of the soldiers stared in horror.

Then, finally, Doctor Tamah stood up and walked into the dimmed light. Her skin was gray and covered with cuts and gashes caked with dry blood. She had blood-red pupils as she stared at them.

She smiled with blood all over her face.

DOCTOR TAMAH
"Change, Captain! Change is what transpired!"

ABOUT THE AUTHOR

Shavor D. Morrison

As a kid growing up with my little brother, we always found ourselves in trouble, grounded to our rooms. The silver lining was that my little brother and I shared the same room! Where we spent most of our "sentences" (no pun intended) making and creating comics, novels, short stories, and picture books! I've been writing for a long time; however, it never dawned on me to share it with the world. So here I am, a guy born and raised in Omaha, NE, who helped create Infinity Universe Entertainment. It presents a lifetime of fantastic storytelling and art! That comes straight from a special place in our hearts! AND! I couldn't have done this without the accompaniment of my little brother, the encouragement of my beautiful and virtuous wife, and inspiration from my three equally amazing and intelligent kids!

THANK YOU!

THANK YOU FOR PURCHASING THIS PROJECT AND TAKING THE TIME TO INDULGE AND GET LOST IN OUR IMAGINATIONS! CONTINUE TO READ AND DREAM, SPEAKING THINGS INTO EXISTENCE!!! ESPECIALLY WHEN THE OPPORTUNITIES ARE INFINITE!!!